For Mamita,
the love of my life.

Dial Books for Young Readers
An imprint of Penguin Random House LLC, New York

First published in the United States of America by Dial Books for Young Readers,
an imprint of Penguin Random House LLC, 2023

Copyright © 2023 by Teresa Nicole L. Yulo

Visit us online at penguinrandomhouse.com.

Library of Congress Cataloging-in-Publication Data is available.

Manufactured in China

ISBN 9780593353875

10 9 8 7 6 5 4 3 2 1

TOPL

Design by Lily Malcom

Text is hand lettered by Nicole L. Yulo

The art for this book was created digitally.

OUT of the BLUE

Nic Yulo

"Ready for the field trip, Coral?"

"You'll be fine."

"Everyone is going."

Dial Books For Young Readers

Coral dreams of going on GRAND adventures.
The world is so BIG and there are SO MANY
things she wants to SEE.

But Coral is SMALL.

The SMALLEST. Some days she

wondered if anyone saw her at all.

It's hard not to feel invisible ...

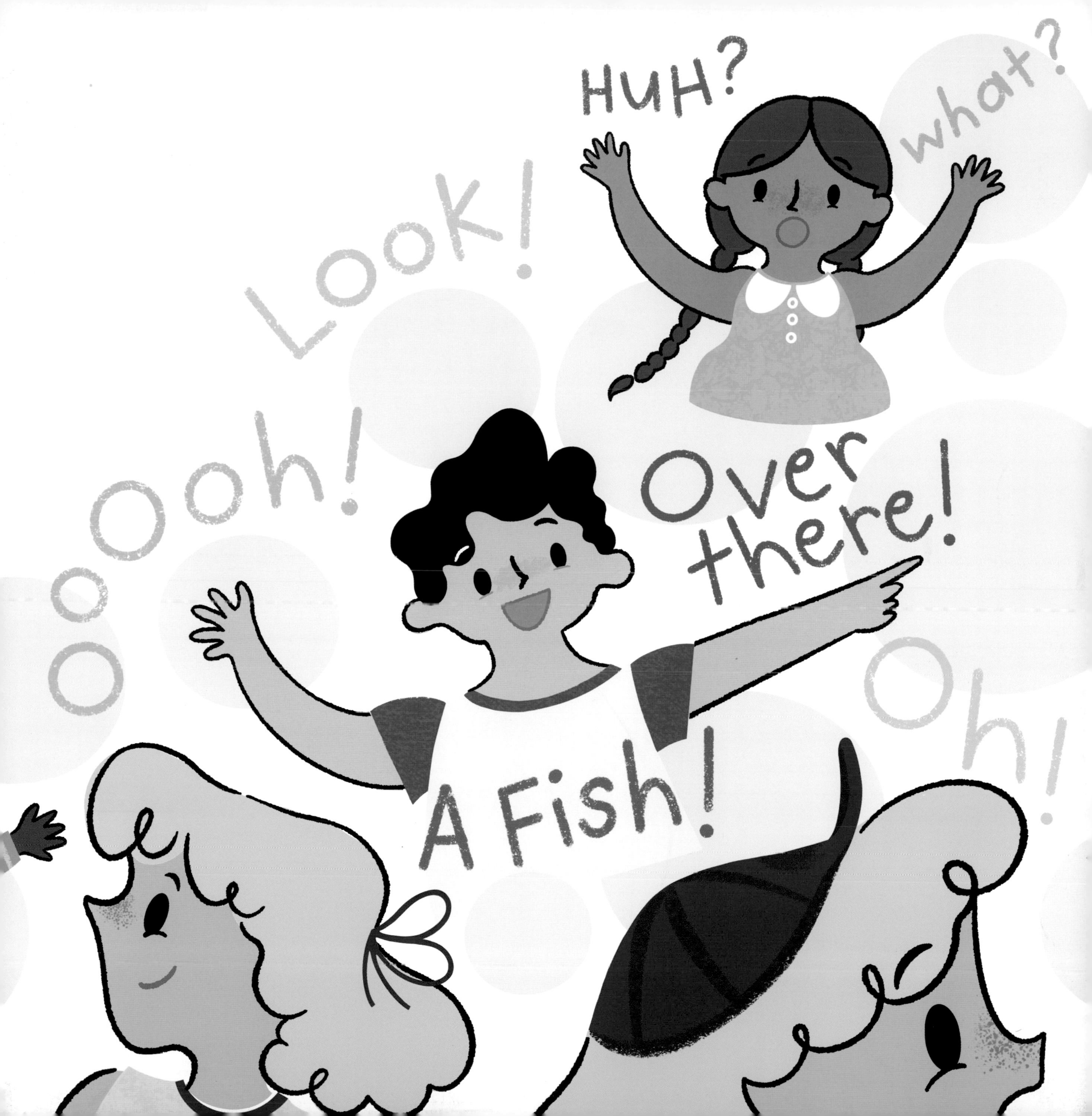
HUH?
what?
Look!
Ooooh!
Over there!
A Fish!
Oh!

...when everything is so much

BIGGER than you.

OL!

BIOLUMINESCENCE HALL

QUIET PLEASE

There's nothing there.

Looks empty.

BOO

TAP
TAP TAP

"I can't see."

With her classmates gone, at least Coral could get some PEACE and QUIET.

NNNN

But now,
not only was she invisible,
she was ALONE.

And who can tell what LURKS in the DARK.

Kraken is SMALL.

Bioluminescent
EXHIBIT

The SMALLEST.

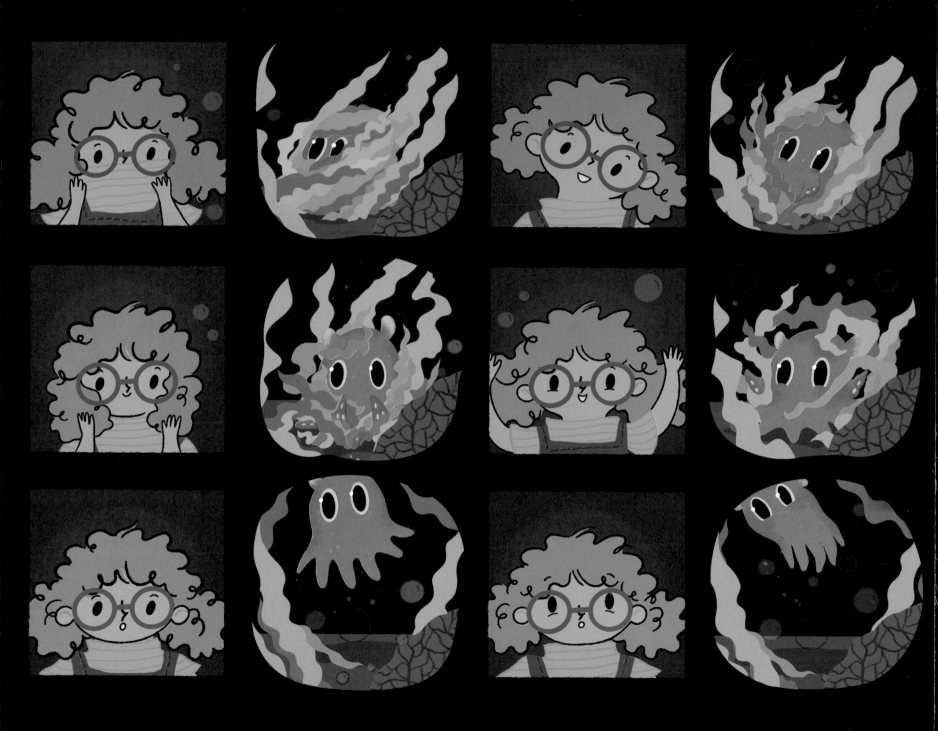

He liked being invisible.
He was GOOD at it.

Being INVISIBLE
can have its PERKS.

"You don't like the noise either, do you?"

The light in his tank helped Kraken see a great many things.

Now Coral could see them too. And it is hard not to get excited...

...When everything is so much

BIGGER than YOU!

WOOOOOOOOOOOOOOOW

From the LIGHT in Kraken's tank,
Coral could SEE a great many things.
Now her classmates could see them TOO.

And it's hard not

to get excited...

...when the WORLD is so much

Big enough for even